WARNING!

Scaredy Squirrel insists that
everyone brush their teeth
with germ-fighting toothpaste
before reading this book.

For my dentist, Rosa, and for Manuel
Special thanks to Valerie, my friend and publisher,
for seven inspiring years

Kids Can Press acknowledges the financial support of the Government of Ontario, through the Ontario Media Development Corporation's Ontario Book Initiative; the Ontario Arts Council; the Canada Council for the Arts; and the Government of Canada, through the BPIDP, for our publishing activity.

Published in Canada by
Kids Can Press Ltd.
29 Birch Avenue
Toronto, ON M4V 1E2

Published in the U.S. by
Kids Can Press Ltd.
2250 Military Road
Tonawanda, NY 14150

www.kidscanpress.com

The artwork in this book was rendered in charcoal pencil and acrylic.
The text is set in Potato Cut.

Edited by Tara Walker
Designed by Mélanie Watt and Karen Powers
Printed and bound in China

This book is smyth sewn casebound.

CM 07 0 9 8 7 6 5 4 3 2 1

LIBRARY AND ARCHIVES CANADA CATALOGUING IN PUBLICATION

Watt, Mélanie, 1975–
    Scaredy squirrel makes a friend / written and illustrated by Mélanie Watt.

ISBN-13: 978-1-55453-181-3   ISBN-10: 1-55453-181-0

1. Squirrels—Juvenile fiction. I. Title.

PS8645.A8845284 2007   jC813'.6   C2006-904829-0

Kids Can Press is a [corus]™ Entertainment company

Scaredy Squirrel

makes a friend

by Mélanie Watt

KIDS CAN PRESS

So Scaredy Squirrel
finds interesting ways
to pass the time all
by himself.

He reads.

He whistles.

He crafts.

He yawns.

Scaredy Squirrel doesn't have a friend.
He'd rather be alone than risk encountering
someone dangerous. A squirrel could get bitten.

A few individuals
Scaredy Squirrel
is afraid to be
bitten by:

walruses

bunnies

beavers

piranhas

Godzilla

He knits.

He chats.

He counts.

Until one day he spots . . .

goldfish

Someone perfectly safe!

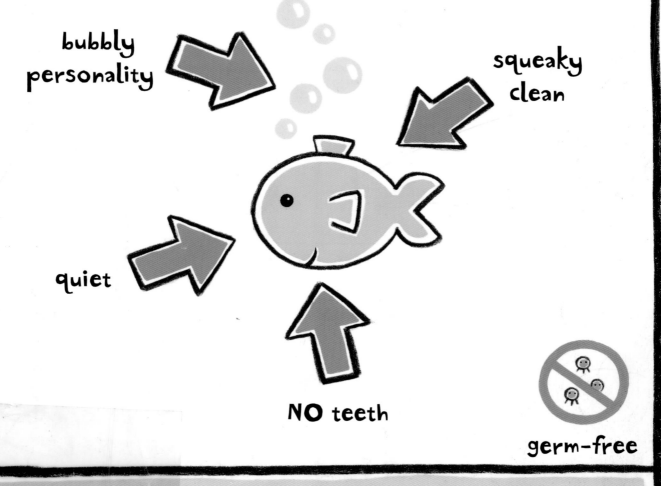

A few items Scaredy Squirrel needs to make the Perfect Friend:

lemon

name tag

mittens

comb

mirror

air freshener

toothbrush

chew toy

How to make the Perfect First Impression:

tame bad hair

brush teeth thoroughly
and practice smile
(check for nutty breath
and food caught
between teeth)

prepare
freshly
squeezed
lemonade

wear mittens
to hide
sweaty paws

HELLO
my name is
Scaredy

make sure
name tag
is visible

use pine scent
to smell
delightful

follow the Perfect Plan ⇨

The Perfect Plan

Step 1: Toss down chew toy to distract biters

Step 2: Use mirror to check hair and teeth

Step 3: Run to fountain

Step 4: Point to name tag and smile

Step 5: Offer lemonade

Step 6: Make the Perfect Friend

Legend

 nut tree

 fountain

 tree

 rocks

 bush

 pine tree

 pond

 biter

 biter

 biter

biter

biter

I am here.

Don't talk to suspicious bunnies.

Stay away from piranha-infested ponds.

Beware of walruses: they're fast on their flippers.

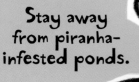

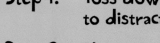

Goldfish is here.

Avoid beavers: they could snap at any moment.

Watch out for Godzilla — for obvious reasons!

BUT let's say, just for example, that Scaredy Squirrel **DID** come face to face with a potential biter. He knows exactly what **NOT** to do . . .

 **DO NOT** show fear.

 **DO NOT** show your fingers.

 **DO NOT** make eye contact.

 **DO NOT** make any loud noises.

 If all else fails, **PLAY DEAD** ...

And hand over the Test.

Scaredy's Risk Test

1) Who are you?

☐   ☐

☐   ☐

☐ other ☐

2) How many teeth do you have?

2 ☐   100 ☐

10 ☐   1000 ☐

32 ☐   more ☐

3) What's your hobby?

biting ☐

other ☐

4) What do you see?

friend ☐   something to bite ☐

And he realizes . . .

The dog chases Scaredy around the bush . . .

around the fountain . . .

Time out!

and around in circles . . .

until Scaredy Squirrel . . .

Plays DEAD.

30 minutes later

1 hour later

2 hours later

After all this time, Scaredy Squirrel realizes that the dog doesn't want to bite him ...

He just wants a friend!

Scaredy Squirrel points to his name tag and smiles.

Then he starts chasing his new buddy.

They play fetch.

They play hide-and-seek.

And they play dead.

Scaredy Squirrel forgets all about the goldfish, not to mention the walruses, bunnies, beavers, piranhas and Godzilla.

Time flies when you're having fun!

All this excitement inspires Scaredy Squirrel to make a few minor changes to his idea of a friend . . .

My Almost Perfect Friend
(according to Scaredy Squirrel)

wet doggy smell

muddy paws

tooth

loud bark

germs

drool

83% safe, but LOTS OF FUN!

P.S. As for the
wet doggy smell,
it's been taken care of.